This book belongs to:

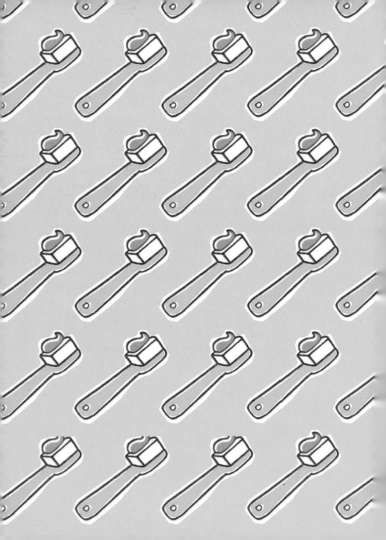

WARNING!

Scaredy Squirrel insists that everyone brush their teeth with germ-fighting toothpaste before reading this book.

For my dentist, Rosa, and for Manuel

Adapted from: *Scaredy Squirrel Makes a Friend*

Text and illustrations © 2007 Mélanie Watt

All rights reserved.
Printed in China. THL

Printed in agreement with Kids Can Press Ltd.,
25 Dockside Drive, Toronto, ON M5A 0B5

www.kidscanpress.com

©2017 McDonald's. The Golden Arches logo, McDonald's and Happy Meal
are trademarks of McDonald's Corporation and its affiliates, licensed to
McDonald's Restaurants of Canada Limited.

Scaredy Squirrel
makes a friend

by Mélanie Watt

KIDS CAN PRESS

Scaredy Squirrel doesn't have a friend. He'd rather be alone than risk encountering someone dangerous. A squirrel could get bitten.

A few individuals Scaredy Squirrel is afraid to be bitten by:

walruses

bunnies

beavers

piranhas

Godzilla

So Scaredy Squirrel finds interesting ways to pass the time all by himself.

He reads.

He crafts.

He whistles.

He yawns.

He knits.

He counts.

He chats.

Until one day
he spots ...

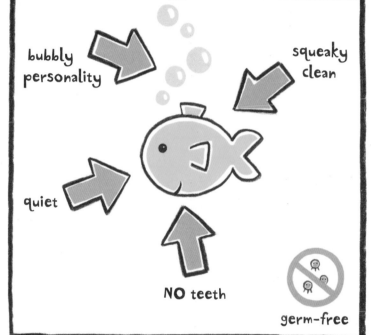

A few items Scaredy Squirrel needs to make the Perfect Friend:

lemon

name tag

mirror

air freshener

... follow the Perfect Plan! ⇨

The Perfect Plan

Step 1: Toss down chew toy to distract biters

Step 2: Use mirror to check hair and teeth

Step 3: Run to fountain

Step 4: Point to name tag and smile

Step 5: Offer lemonade

Step 6: Make the Perfect Friend

I am here. ✗

Legend

🌰 nut tree
💧 fountain
🌳 tree
🪨 rocks
🌿 bush
🌲 pine tree
⬭ pond
🦒 biter
🐰 biter
🐿 biter
🐟 biter
🦎 biter

Stay away from piranha-infested ponds.

Beware of walruses: they're fast on their flippers.

Don't talk to suspicious bunnies.

Goldfish
is here.

Avoid beavers:
they could
snap at any
moment.

Watch out for Godzilla —
for obvious reasons!

BUT let's say,
just for example,
that Scaredy
Squirrel DID come
face to face with
a potential biter.
He knows exactly
what NOT to do ...

 **DO NOT** show fear.

 DO NOT show your fingers.

 **DO NOT** make eye contact.

 **DO NOT** make any loud noises.

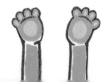 If all else fails, **PLAY DEAD** ...

And hand over the Test.

With every detail under control, Scaredy Squirrel puts the Plan into action.

First he tosses the chew toy.

Then he heads down the tree.

Everything is perfect until he hears a strange sound coming from behind:

SQUEEEAK!

And he realizes . . .

The dog chases Scaredy around the bush . . .

around the fountain . . .

Time out!

and around in circles . . .

until Scaredy Squirrel . . .

Plays DEAD.

30 minutes later

1 hour later

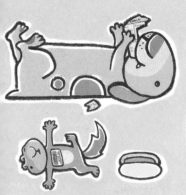

2 hours later

After all this time,
Scaredy Squirrel
realizes that the
dog doesn't want
to bite him ...

He just wants a friend!

Scaredy Squirrel points to his name tag and smiles.

Then he starts chasing his new buddy.

They play fetch.

They play hide-and-seek.

And they play dead.

Scaredy Squirrel forgets all about the goldfish, not to mention the walruses, bunnies, beavers, piranhas and Godzilla.

Time flies when you're having fun!

All this excitement inspires Scaredy Squirrel to make a few minor changes to his idea of a friend ...

P.S. As for the wet doggy smell, it's been taken care of.

fresh flower scent

ACTIVITIES

Make-a-Friend Kit

Can you think of SIX items that might help you make a new friend? Draw them here.

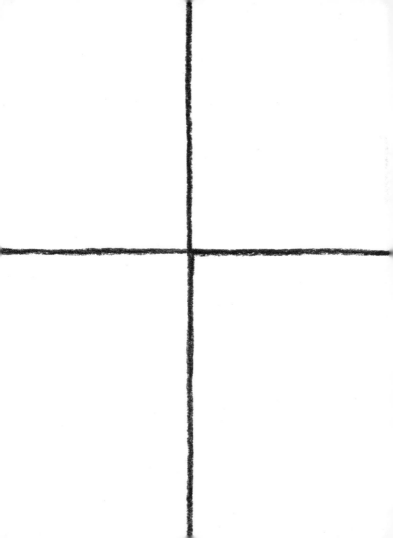

Matching Fun

Scaredy Squirrel finds lots of ways to pass the time all by himself. Can you match each of these words with one picture on the opposite page? Write out the word below each picture.

whistling

reading

crafting

yawning

counting

knitting

_____

_____

_____

_____

_____

_____

Connect the Dots

Connect the dots from 1 to 20 to find out what Scaredy Squirrel uses to make the perfect first impression.

ould you make the perfect friend for Scaredy? To find out,
l out this test. Then check your answers on the next page.

Scaredy's Risk Test

Age:

Name:

1) Who are you?

a) ☐ d) ☐

b) ☐ e) ☐

c) ☐ f) other ☐

2) How many teeth do you have (approx.)?

a) 2 ☐   d) 100 ☐

b) 20 ☐ e) 1000 ☐

c) 32 ☐ f) more ☐

3) What's your hobby?

a) biting ☐

b) other ☐ : _____

_____

4) What do you see?

a) friend ☐   b) something ☐ to bite

Answers

Matching Fun

knitting   reading

whistling   yawning

counting   crafting

Connect the Dots

Scaredy's Risk Test

If you scored 3 points or more, you'd make a great friend for Scaredy!

1) a-e: 0 points
   f: 1 point

2) a: 3 points
   b: 2 points
   c: 1 point
   d-f: 0 points

3) a: 0 points
   b: 1 point

4) a: 1 point
   b: 0 points